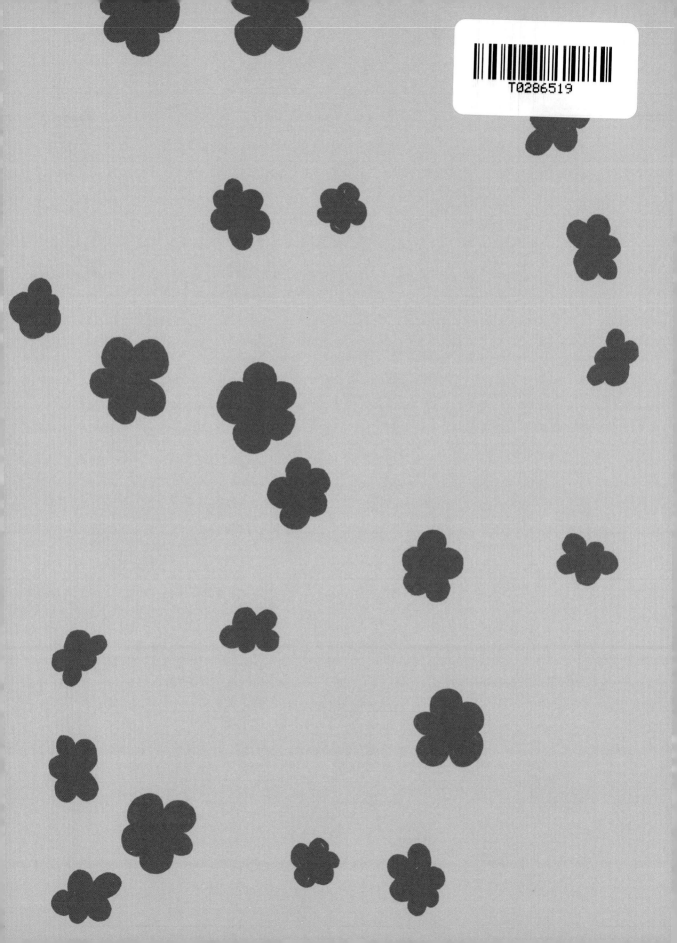

For Marius and Adrian

PUSHKIN PRESS
71–75 Shelton Street
London WC2H 9JQ

ORIGINAL TITLE *Fisens Liv*
TEXT © Malin Klingenberg, 2019
ILLUSTRATIONS & GRAPHIC DESIGN © Sanna Mander, 2019
ENGLISH TRANSLATION © A.A. Prime, 2020

Published by agreement with Helsinki Literary Agency

Published originally in Swedish by Schildts & Söderströms
First published by Pushkin Press in 2020

1 3 5 7 9 8 6 4 2

ISBN 13: 978-1-78269-283-6

This work has been published
with the financial assistance of FILI –
Finnish Literature Exchange

Printed by Livonia Print, Latvia

WWW.PUSHKINPRESS.COM

MALIN KLINGENBERG

illustrated by

SANNA MANDER

THE SECRET LIFE OF FARTS

Translated by
A.A. Prime

Pushkin
Children's

The life of a fart is tragically short
So let's take a moment and spare them a thought
Farts can feel lonely once out of the bum
But amazing adventures are waiting for some

Like the fart that was born in the high mountain peaks
And slipped out between a rock climber's cheeks
For one happy moment it smelled like Swiss cheese
Then the stench disappeared in the fresh Alpine breeze

Did you hear of the fart that took part in a race?
And not only that – it won second place!
The Olympics are great, but I think it's a shame
That farts don't get medals or glory or fame

There once was a diver who let out a guff
But her wetsuit, alas, was not tight enough
A big bubble billowed but didn't disperse
Till it rose all the way to the surface and burst

When a robber broke into a kitchen one day
He retched at the reek and scuttled away
For the panicking chef hadn't known what to do
And had let out a stinker, like rotten fondue

HOTEL

RECEPTION
LIFT →
LOBBY →

Reception

Upper-class types with plenty of money
Pass wind discreetly and don't find it funny
Their well-trained releases are usually silent
But the stenches created are often quite violent

A serial farter found farts so amusing
She laughed in a lift where her farts were diffusing
Her parps were melodic and made up a tune
A tune about farting, played on the bassoon

Kings and queens even know how it feels
And relish a gut-bubble after big meals
There once was a tsar who conquered a nation
With a specially odorous bottom vibration

To break wind is silent, a civil affair
To let rip is noisy, so farter beware!
A toot or a blow, a honk or a squeak
Each fart is special, each fart is unique

Botty pops putter like guns in a war
While trumps just explode in an almighty roar
Guffs tend to stink like a punch in the nose
While daintier puffs are absorbed into clothes

They say that beans are the musical fruit
But you've never heard music like THIS guy can toot
Throughout his career the maestro grew rich
From his gases so perfect in rhythm and pitch

A girl who loved milkshakes and drank without care
Soon found herself rocket-launched into the air
A genius invention – an eco solution:
'Gas-powered flights without the pollution!'

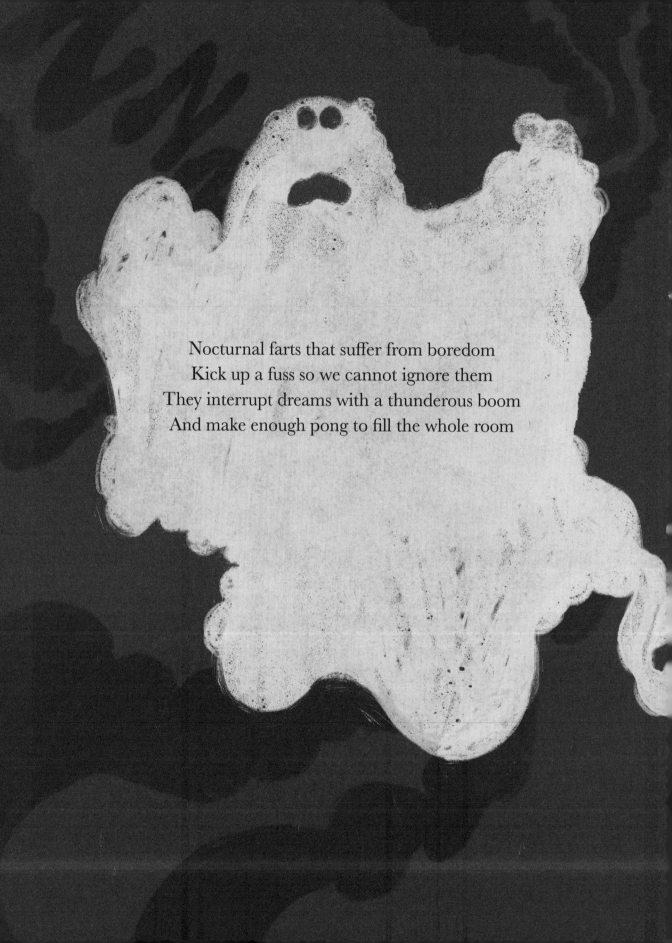

Nocturnal farts that suffer from boredom
Kick up a fuss so we cannot ignore them
They interrupt dreams with a thunderous boom
And make enough pong to fill the whole room

There's not often time for a fart to make friends
One moment to shine, then its lonely life ends
But they stand a good chance at a middle-aged party
When grown-ups get going, they often get farty

One lucky fart was released into space
And drifted through darkness with dignified grace
It floated out freely past Venus and Mars
To join fellow gases exploding in stars

Although farts are smelly and sometimes seem rude
A well-timed expulsion can lighten the mood
Joking aside, it's often quite smart
To laugh good and long at a farcical fart

Grown-ups and grannies and children and teens
Goodies and baddies and those in between
Each person with brains and a spine and a heart
and guts and a bottom – loves a good fart

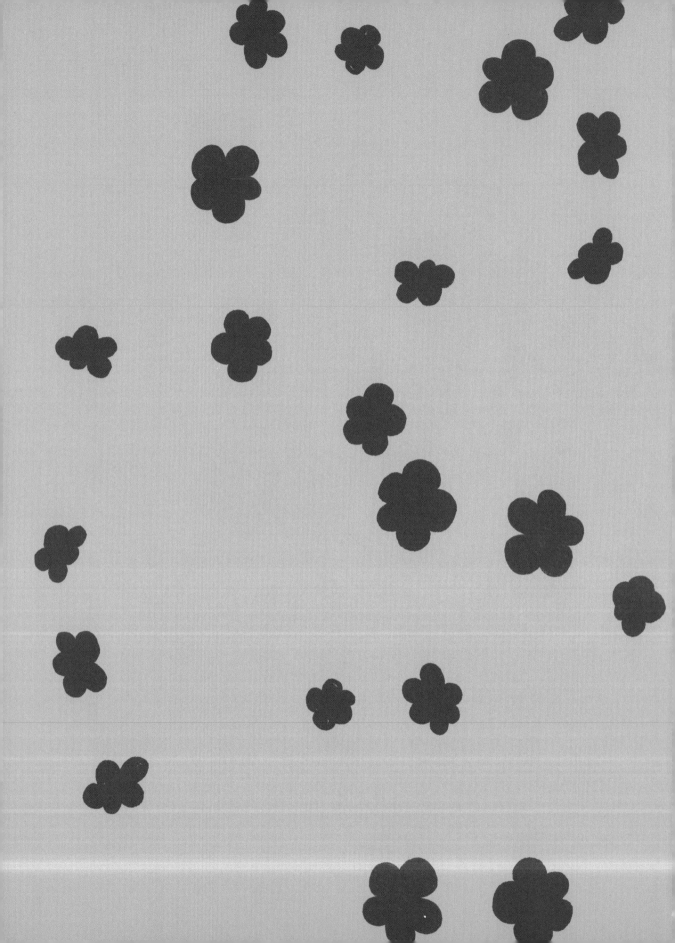